Nightmare Store

PLOT-YOUR-OWN
HORROR STORIES ™ #2

Nightmare Store

By HILARY MILTON

WANDERER BOOKS
Published by Simon & Schuster, New York

Copyright© 1982 by Hilary Milton
Published by WANDERER BOOKS
A Simon & Schuster Division of
Gulf & Western Corporation
Simon & Schuster Building
1230 Avenue of the Americas
New York, New York 10020

Designed by Stanley S. Drate

Manufactured in the United States of America

10 9 8 7 6 5 4 3

WANDERER and colophon are trademarks
of Simon & Schuster
Library of Congress Cataloging in Publication Data

Milton, Hilary H.
    Nightmare store.

    (Plot your own horror stories; 2)
    Summary: The reader, trapped after closing in the newest and
largest department store in Atlanta, is given choices to make to
remove himself from the night of terror.
    [1. Department stores—Fiction. 2. Horror—Fiction. 3. Literary
recreations] I. Title. II. Series.
PZ7.M6447Ni   [Fic]   82–7027
ISBN 0–671–45630–X   AACR2

BEWARE!

Wallenberg's is filled with unspeakable evil. You'll struggle desperately to find your way out of this nightmare's many terrors. Don't read straight through, however, as almost every page holds bewildering choices that have to be made.

Should or shouldn't you follow the chilling noise?
If you enter the tiny dark room, will you be trapped
     forever?
If you turn the corner, will the evil creature be
     waiting there . . . hungry?

Remember, your fate is in your own hands. Only you can decide whether or not you'll make it through the many tales of horror in Nightmare Store!

Going shopping for yourself, all on your own, is something quite new and different for you. Home is a small town in Mississippi, not far from the Tombigbee River, but this week you're visiting your aunt and uncle, Louise and Jerry Hardesty, in Atlanta. For the past three days they have taken you all over the city, showing you where the Falcons play football, Underground Atlanta, Six Flags over Georgia, Jungle Land, and even Stone Mountain.

Tonight, however, Uncle Jerry has a short meeting with some of his company's officials from out of town, and Aunt Louise is at the hospital, visiting a friend who was injured in an automobile accident. Uncle Jerry suggests that instead of staying home by yourself, you spend the evening in Wallenberg's, the newest and largest department store in Atlanta. And, to make it more interesting, he has given you money to buy something for yourself and a gift to take back to your younger brother.

Going shopping by yourself, you discover, is more than just a little fun. Nobody says "Let's go to the dress shop," nobody says "Let's go look at men's shoes or suits," and nobody tells you not to handle any of the items on display.

1

2

Oh, it's fun.

And Wallenberg's is an especially good place to have fun in. It's huge, much larger than any store back home. In fact, as you walk from section to section, and from floor to floor, you have the feeling that this store has even more departments than all the stores back home, even if they were under one roof.

You look at clothes, you wander through the model rooms of furniture, and then you ride the escalator downstairs to the really interesting departments—sporting goods and clothing. In one large area, you see tents, camping equipment, inflatable rafts, fishing gear, all sorts of athletic training devices, and even skiing outfits. You can't help smiling when you see those—who can ski in Atlanta?

You linger at the section where the camping equipment is because you think Ray, your little brother, might like a camp stool—he's always moving chairs around so he can sit where he wants to.

After looking at everything carefully, you finally ride the escalator all the way to the fourth floor. Off to one end is a display of television sets and you wander in that direction. This place is not like any television display area you have ever been in before. Instead of having rows and rows of sets, all tuned to the same station, these are arranged in groups, three to each location, with comfortable chairs where would-be purchasers can sit and watch the shows. That, you decide, is the best way to look. You can truly see how the different sets perform.

A clerk walks over while you're standing beside a deep brown lounger and asks if you don't want to sit down. "You'll enjoy the program better that way," she says.

You thank her and sink down in the huge recliner. You lean back and watch for a while. However, you've been walking much more than usual and you're tired. You don't intend to, but you fall asleep.

And nobody wakes you up!

When you wake up on your own, the television sets are off, and almost all of the store's lights are out, with only the low safety ones glowing softly. And nobody, but nobody, is around.

You turn around, dumbfounded for a minute, then you hold your wrist up to look at the time. Fifteen minutes after ten—and Uncle Jerry said he'd pick you up at nine-thirty!

You spring from the chair and start to run toward the escalator—only to trip over a footstool that you hadn't noticed earlier. You get up, try to see through the murky darkness, and move more slowly toward the escalator. You step onto the moving staircase,

4

only to learn that it has stopped running. Well, no wonder. When the store closes, all the electrical equipment is turned off.

Within ten minutes, you have walked all the way down to the main floor and felt your way toward the office—you remember where it is because you passed it going from the boot department toward the escalator earlier. You can call Aunt Louise; she ought to be at home by now, and she can have Uncle Jerry come pick you up.

But the office is locked tight.

You know there are telephones at the various department counters, however, so you feel your way to the nearest one, in the ladies' cosmetics section. You find the telephone and lift it from its cradle— only to find that it is dead.

Somebody has cut off the telephones.

The idea scares you for a moment, until you decide that the office staff must have a master switch, a way of turning off the telephones when the store closes.

No matter.

You'll just walk out the front door and use a pay phone.

Except you can't get the door open. And when you push on the long brass handle it makes a buzz. You jump back, wondering if it's a burglar alarm or an electrical device that would shock you if you held it too long.

You vaguely remember seeing a phone booth on the second floor, right outside the rest rooms, so you climb the escalator once more.

But this time something you hadn't expected happens. You're halfway up when the escalator begins to move! Oh, no—it's going down!

You try to run, thinking you can go faster than the stairway. But the faster you run, the faster it moves. Finally, almost out of breath, you turn around and just go with the stairs. Now when you're only ten steps from the bottom, it suddenly stops, then begins to carry you up once more. Fast, faster, even faster! As it reaches the second-floor level you leap clear— just before it reverses itself and begins to descend again.

And now you really are beginning to get frightened. You know there must be a fire escape, some way for people to leave the upper floors when the power goes off or if there's a fire, but you haven't the slightest idea where it is. You can go look for it, knowing that it will probably take you a long time to find it, or you can just find a comfortable place to sit and go back to sleep until morning.

If you decide to look for the fire escape, turn to page 11.
If you decide to find a place to sit and sleep,
turn to page 20.

6

You can't believe it, but the alligator is coming up the escalator, too. Its very short legs and strong clawlike toes catch on the individual steps, and its powerful tail pushes it upward. While you can run faster than it can crawl, you have the uneasy feeling that it's much smarter than an ordinary alligator.

You reach the top of the first flight and hesitate a moment, then you scurry to the second flight. When you get there, you pause long enough to catch your breath.

And you listen hard.

The alligator also went around the narrow wall and is now on the second flight of stairs. And by its thumping noises you are positive that it's even bigger than when you first spied it.

The safety lights are so dim here that you can barely make out shadows. But you're able to see just enough to know you're on the floor with men's and boys' clothing and the rest rooms.

Hey, the rest rooms!

If you can get the creature to follow you to the rest rooms you can get him inside and trap him—lock him in while he's trying to turn around. You're sure he'll follow you.

It might not be such a great idea after all, you admit to yourself. The rest rooms might be locked.

If you decide to keep climbing, turn to page 25.
If you decide to trap the alligator, turn to page 73.

When you hear the noise again, you quickly make up your mind. A burglar breaking into this big store would certainly have a gun, and if he sees you he won't ask questions—he'll just shoot.

The safest place, you think, would be the big chair near the TVs—the same place you were sleeping.

It takes a few minutes to find the escalator, but once you locate it you race all the way to the fourth floor. You are out of breath but away from whatever the source of the noise is. You reach the TV section, find the same chair, and wearily sink into it. You slump against the soft cushions and start to close your eyes.

7

Does the burglar show up? Turn to page 42.
Or does something else frighten you? Turn to page 112.

8

You are suddenly terrified—because you believe you know why the wide tunnel leads downhill. Trash and empty boxes are brought here, and dumped into a raging open furnace.

You scream. You dig in your toes. You grab at the soft cement but it's like mush, and all you feel is gritty, wet sand and bits of gravel.

Your foot catches and for a moment you believe there's something to hold you back. But the foot slips off and now you're going faster and faster.

You flail wildly with both arms. You push with your hands. You kick your legs. But nothing stops your speeding slide.

You come to the end of the tunnel and your arms are now swinging loosely over hot blowing air. And before you can do anything more than scream and scream, you slide over the edge.

Down and down toward the roaring flames . . .

THE END

Summoning all your will and strength, you whirl about and begin to run. You knock over a table containing knives and sharpening tools, you bang against a rack of hunting boots and shelves of socks, you crack your shin on a low exercise bench and trip over it.

9

Scrambling to your feet, you spin around as you rise to see if the creatures are still where you last saw them. They are not, and the clacking noises you hear are their plastic feet, skittering over the tile floor. Something whizzes past your ear and bores into a far cabinet, splitting the wood. The fishing spear—it has to be the fishing spear.

You drop to your knees, shouting at them to leave you alone.

Your hand finds a diver's flipper and you turn to hurl it at them. It strikes the hunter in the head—and the head explodes! At once, another head takes the first one's place. You tremble all over but dare not stop.

Standing up again, you start running faster. Once more you hear something zing past your head. It thuds against a sleeping bag, and you know the climber has thrown his knife. You cry out, stop abruptly, and spin about.

Maybe if you charge into them—

Turn to page 10.

10

But before you can move, you see the climber twirling his tether rope as a cowboy might twirl a lasso. He aims it toward you and swings it in a swift arc. It drops about your shoulders, but before it can be drawn tight, you wriggle free. You wildly feel about for something else to hurl at them. Your hand touches something cold and hard and you know it's a small hatchet. Your fingers slip to the handle, you clasp it firmly, pause, then throw it with all your might.

It strikes the diver first, knocking off the snorkel. It bounces from that mannequin to the climber, cutting through the tether and slicing away the creature's heavy belt.

Once more it bounces up, this time coming down on the hunter's bow. It severs the string, becomes entangled and swings upward, hitting the figure in the throat.

Something gushes out but you can't tell what it is—except that it has an awful smell.

Then the hatchet rises as if drawn up by an invisible cord. It whirls and whirls and whirls above the mannequins' forms and you are hypnotized by it.

And you are not able to move at all when it suddenly ceases to whirl, turns toward you blade first, and whistles eerily through the foul-smelling air as it heads directly for your chest. . . .

THE END

The idea of spending the whole night in the store doesn't appeal to you because you're beginning to believe something weird is going on inside. The fire escape will let you out, and you can call Aunt Louise.

As you think back over all your wanderings, you decide that the rear part of the store is the probable location of the fire escape. So you carefully work your way through long racks of dresses and coats. Once you glance to the left and you suddenly freeze. A woman is standing right there, staring at you. Cold chills run up and down your spine before you suddenly remember that mannequins are all over the place. You chide yourself for being afraid and continue through the racks.

Several minutes later, you bump into a mirror— you've come to the dressing room area. You are about to turn to the left when you hear a strange noise.

You try to guess what it is but finally you give up. You turn to the right away from the mirror and feel your way along the wall until it abruptly stops. You take another step and find you're in an open area. You turn left and hurry toward the building's rear wall.

As you pass a small counter, you look up and see what you believe is a big glass EXIT sign. You think the smaller words say "For Emergency Use." You find a double door with long handles and push

Turn to page 12.

12

against them. They catch for a moment, then suddenly give way, and you're out of the women's clothing department. You step onto the uncarpeted concrete landing at the top of the stairs. The door jerks away from your hand and slams shut. And you cannot open it!

Well, never mind. You're on your way out.

You peer through the darkness as you try to make out the stairway; there is a small safety light at the bottom but it gives very little light.

You feel your way down, taking each step slowly. You are about a quarter of the way down when you have a frightening realization: the farther down you go, the narrower the steps seem to be getting, and you wonder about the people who designed this building. Steps should be the same width—

Turn to page 24.

In the darkness you can't tell how long the creature is, but you are certain it is at least eight feet long and still growing. Its gigantic mouth opens and closes in slow motion, and its small, glinting eyes are fixed on you, as if the creature considers you a perfect midnight meal.

13

You swallow and choke and try to spin about, but your feet won't behave. For a brief moment all you are able to do is stand there, only a couple of feet from the monster as its wide, bladelike tail swishes back and forth. Its jaws seem to be wide enough to take you in with one giant bite.

Turn to page 15.

15

As you continue to stand paralyzed, its broad body begins to move in your direction, the small legs padding right and left as they propel the creature. Finally, your feet obey your mind and you spin about—only to crash headlong into a fixed, heavy stand in the middle of the aisle, the store's floor layout and department directory.

You try to climb up on it, but in your haste you catch your foot on a wide guardrail around the stand. You fall forward, your feet only inches away from the gator's busily working jaws. And you know that you must either stay there and try to fight off the creature or roll as rapidly as you can toward one of the cosmetics displays.

If you choose to fight the alligator, turn to page 92.
If you decide to roll away, turn to page 86.

16

While you cannot see well in the faint light, the three mannequins seem to glow with a kind of yellow-green light.

Trembling, you try to look into their faces. But they have no faces. Their heads are covered with wigs but where eyes and noses and mouths should be, there are only rounded shapes.

You slip one foot to the left, act as if you mean to run, and start to crouch for a good start. At once all the weapons are aimed directly at your head. You freeze with your arms clamped to your sides.

You hear noises, low guttural noises coming from one, then the other of them. The sounds are so deep, you presume they come from the males, but when you glance in their direction, the hunter is ignoring the other two. The female diver has the same kind of deep-throated voice.

If they're speaking words, you cannot understand them. However, you have the eerie feeling that they *are* conversing and their conversation concerns you. You wish you knew what they are saying.

After several moments, the female takes a slow, awkward step toward you and you believe they've come to some kind of decision.

If you believe the female will attack you alone, turn to page 116.
If you think the hunter will attack, turn to page 39.
If you expect the attacker to be the climber, turn to page 96.

But before you've had time to do more than take a deep breath, something beneath you begins to move—to vibrate. Part of the padding beneath you rises and curls around your left side, then some to your right. Before you can do anything more than gasp you're being wrapped over and over again in the padding.

17

And that's what it is—padding used to ship large items. Within seconds you're completely enclosed in the stuff and you can barely breathe.

Turn to page 119.

18

the long tether rope and wraps it around both the column and you. Within seconds, you are bound to the structure. When the thing releases you, there is the distinct, though hoarse, sound of laughter.

It backs its way to the floor and retreats to a point twenty feet from the column, and it throws aside its heavy coat. And now, in addition to the one knife it holds in its hand, you see the hilts of nine more.

Its featureless face fixes on you and it raises the knife. Its arm swings, you see a brief flash, and a blade strikes the column half an inch from your right cheek. Again the sound.

The hand grabs another blade, draws back, arcs forward. And this one buries itself in the column half an inch from your left cheek. You scream, but there is little you can do other than kick and flail your arms.

Seven more times the arm swings toward you. Seven more knives are buried in the column—to the right of your stomach, to the left of it, beside your left ankle, beside your right, one between your thighs, one under your left arm, and one under your right.

There is only one knife left.

The arm raises itself, set at an angle with the knife caught in the plastic fingers. This time, as the blade arcs toward you, you wildly grab out, knowing this one is aimed at your heart. Miraculously, your fingers

Continue.

catch the hilt just before the point touches your flesh. Again you scream out and hurl the blade back at the mannequin.

19

And like another miracle, its sharp point finds its mark—the center of the mannequin's chest.

The roaring, screeching, screaming sound that comes from the creature is unlike any noise you've ever heard. The creature staggers against a counter, slowly fixes its featureless face on you—

Except that now it is not featureless. It has taken on a nose, a mouth, eyes, and a forehead that make it look exactly like Uncle Jerry. . . .

THE END

20

While you wandered through the store before it closed, you found very few places to sit down, other than the fourth floor where all the furniture and television sets were. But right now you're only on the second floor, and that means you'll have to use the escalators. And if they're like the one you just got off, you wonder whether you'll ever make it.

As you try to get your bearings, you suddenly hear sounds coming from—where? You hold your breath, turning slowly. There—from the escalator well. Cautiously you move to the top of it and lean over. You can't be certain, but it sounds as though somebody is moving boxes.

Hey, that's good—down in the storage section of the very lowest floor—you guess it's the basement—workmen are bringing in new merchandise. If you can catch their attention, they will get you out. You grasp the escalator rail and lean forward. "Help! Somebody, help me!"

You pause and listen but you hear no reply.

"Help!"

Turn to page 46.

With nothing more than a little light at the bottom to guide you, and with no knowledge at all of what you might find there, you whirl about and retrace your steps. You leap the stairs three at a time. You reach the landing and turn toward the door just as the outer wall begins to press against you. For a moment you are panic-stricken, thinking you are locked out. But you put your shoulder against the door and shove as hard as you can. Something in the latchwork gives and the door swings in.

You breathe a quick sigh of relief and close the door behind you.

But something isn't right. Something is horribly wrong with this night, this building. The escalators should be either on and working correctly or off and not moving at all. And that wall—there is no rational explanation for a wall that suddenly begins to move.

If you mean to look for another way out, turn to page 72.
If you suddenly make a new discovery, turn to page 58.

22

You force yourself to stretch both feet until they're well planted on the hearth. You hesitate only a moment, until your arms are in just the right place.

And then with a lunge you shove!

The mannequin's head turns once, and you see that the blank face you remember suddenly has a witch's horrid eyes, mouth, and nose, with deep wrinkles over the cheeks. It lets out a very strange and frightening screech.

Then it tumbles into the flames.

Just as the plastic fingers release their hold on your neck, the flames flare high. The mannequin swells violently, and before you have time to take a single step, it explodes!

As if caught by the full force of a dynamite blast, you are lifted from the hearth and blown like a leaf in a whirlwind across the department store, aiming straight for the huge display window. You are hurled through it, splintering glass and knocking down all the decorations.

Turn to page 120.

Feeling your way along, you head back to the escalator. And when you reach it, you remember that the handrail is mounted on a wide, waist-high wall. If you can't use the steps, then why not climb onto the rail and slide down?

23

You feel the edges, then carefully climb onto the railing, being very cautious about where you put your feet. As you mount it and begin to slide down slowly, you are aware of the sound of splashing water. You decide without much thought that the elaborate decorative fountain you noticed on the main floor of the store has also been turned off for the night and water from the storage tanks must be bubbling back into the fountain's basin.

As you reach the bottom, though, and ease off the railing, the splashing noise becomes much louder. It makes you wonder if somebody else is in the store and has stopped by the fountain to swish the water about. But when you turn fully around so you can peer at it, you stop stock-still and scream.

Earlier this evening there'd been a very docile, very lazy iguana lying on an artificial rock. The iguana has changed. It is not a quiet little creature any longer. Now it is an alligator!

Turn to page 13.

24

Wait, now. The steps weren't built narrower as they descended. Not at all. They are getting narrower *now*. The outer wall is moving in—you're suddenly sure of it because the faint light at the bottom is growing fainter.

You stop abruptly and catch your breath. If the stairway is getting narrower, how long will it take for the walls to press all the way together, crushing the steps—and you.

You can run the rest of the way, hoping you don't fall. Or you can turn around and scurry back to the little landing, break through the door, and escape from whatever the walls here are doing.

If you decide to race to the bottom, turn to page 37.
If you decide to return to the landing, turn to page 21.

You hesitate only a minute before deciding to keep going up the escalators. With only a quick glance back, you believe that if you can get to the fourth floor while the creature is still on the escalator stairs, you can find a place to hide. Scampering around the thick column that supports the next flight of steps, you take them as you did the others—two and three at a time. At the landing you pause briefly, then turn down what you believe to be a wide aisle leading toward the furniture department.

On the way you spot the silhouette of a man!

You stop abruptly—then realize it's only a manne-quin; you vaguely recall seeing it earlier. It is a man dressed in casual clothes and he's standing beside an upright barbecue grill.

Hey, now. If the creature gets this far, maybe it'll mistake the mannequin for you and attack it.

You pause just long enough to ease the statuelike figure into the center of the aisle. Then you proceed onward, on tiptoe now so the alligator won't be able to track you by sound.

You go past dining room suites and through a section of large sofas and chairs, finally reaching an area with mattresses and box springs. You pause a moment, frantically looking for a hiding place.

Under a bed? Turn to page 52.
If you spot something else, turn to page 74.

25

26

But the water does not flow out. Instead, it turns into steam as it escapes, spreading like a cloud throughout the entire area. As soon as the weight is lessened, you scramble to the side and fall on the floor. But as you do, in the dim light you see that one of the coil-snakes has broken through its covering. It spies you and moves toward you, slithering over the floor.

And it is followed by all the others.

You try to run but the steam has so fogged your eyes that you cannot see anything. You bump into a brass bed frame and trip over it. You scramble to your feet and run blindly toward the escalator.

Turn to page 44.

It shifts again, and you know it's growing. Something else—the fur rug you're on is also beginning to move. It seems to be swelling and taking a new shape. The breathing gets louder and louder. You shiver all over, trying to figure out what's happening.

27

The rug begins to vibrate. And before you know what's happened, the thing takes a frightening shape.

Turn to page 53.

28

But the moment your presence is noticed, the sounds stop. The creatures halt in the midst of their dance and spin toward you. And before you can do more than make a coughing sound, the chant begins once more: "Death to Wallies . . . death to Wallies . . . death to them that serve . . . death to them that buy . . . death to Wallies."

Your thoughts race. Wallies? Wallenberg's? Has to be—the chant has to apply to the owners. *And* the people who work in the store. *And* the customers.

You're a customer.

Turn to page 84.

But something doesn't sound exactly right. The bubbling noise isn't clear, the way boiling water ought to sound. It is heavier and deeper, as if the liquid inside were thick, heavy soup.

29

Suddenly, before you can move, the giant urn literally blows its lid off. Steam rises in a thick, brown cloud. Quickly you reach up to clamp the lid back in place.

Before you can do so, however, the contents begin to spill over the top and run down the side. It smells like coffee, but it is thick and tarlike. You involuntarily put your hand up to stop the flow—and it sticks to the urn's side!

You try to pull away, but you cannot. You put the other hand against the side to get leverage and it, too, sticks.

Within half a second the thick, tarry glop is running down your arms, scalding you as it flows. It smothers your shoulders and dribbles down your clothes, covering your body. And as quickly as it covers you, it instantly hardens.

You try to scream, but the glop spills into your mouth, across your cheeks, burning everywhere it touches.

Turn to page 30.

30

And before you can move away, you are totally coated with it. It continues to thicken, to cake—and to harden.

And within another minute, you have become a statue—motionless and breathless. . . .

THE END

You're trapped.

You know that if the mattress continues swelling you'll be suffocated by the sheer weight. It's already making you breathe hard and your chest is beginning to hurt. Also, you think your feet are going to sleep and you can barely move your fingers.

31

If you think about puncturing the water bed,
turn to page 78.
If you want to escape another way,
turn to page 54.

32

But before you have time to breathe a sigh of relief, sparks begin to fly from first one location, then another. And you know what's happened. The water has seeped into the base and floor plugs, where exhibited lamps could be attached. The sparks snap and pop and you're afraid that instead of being squashed by the mattress, you're going to be electrocuted.

You try to scramble away, toward some dry place.

Then you hear it—not very loud but clear and distinct—a fire engine's siren.

Turn to page 57.

You come to a wide aisle and scurry across it, hoping that something will trip the creatures or force them to change direction. When you pause to glance around, you are relieved to see that *Purgot* has stopped. Its head seems to be sinking and half of its huge body is bent over. You are certain its battery has run down and it cannot move.

33

Good, good.

But the skeleton continues coming in your direction, stalking you as a hunter stalks his prey. Its joints rattle one against the other, its bones bump and clatter, and the skull wobbles on the small spinal column. Nothing seems able to stop it.

It is even taller, you think, than it was seconds earlier. And the glow around the eye sockets gleams brighter.

What makes it move? It doesn't have a battery or a visible motor.

But whatever it has, it pursues you.

You crawl all over the floor, bumping into counter legs and display cases. You duck behind a row of large power tools. You work your way through an accumulation of exhaust fans and duct piping.

The skeleton, clack-rattling as it moves, never falters.

You come to a large, square, concrete support post, much larger than any other you've seen. If you

Turn to page 34.

34 can ease behind it, you believe the skeleton will lose sight of you.

It doesn't work.

Even while you're ducking low, making yourself seem a part of the structure, it twists around and stares down at you.

Turn to page 97.

A fourth and a fifth arrow fly near—the last one buzzes, and you wonder if it has a different kind of tip. You drop to the floor, hide behind a counter with all kinds of building items—and you grab at anything you can throw. You find a pair of door hinges that you think you can throw a long distance, but you bump your arm as you try to hurl them and they fall harmlessly in the aisle.

You reach again, but out of the corner of your eye you spot the hunter drawing back his bow once more. He lets the arrow fly—and it crashes with a terrible bang into a large metal trash container—

You are startled awake and suddenly sit up. You're still in the chair, still facing the television set—and you don't believe what's on the screen. A hunter on an African safari stands facing a huge lion. As the beast stalks, the hunter sets his arrow and draws back the powerful string. You hold your breath—

Someone taps you on the shoulder and you spring halfway out of the chair. And only then do you realize that you've gone to sleep, that it's the store's closing time, and that people are all heading for the door.

You sigh with real relief as you slowly climb out of the chair and make your way toward the escalators. But as you start down, you glance off to your right.

Turn to page 36.

35

36

In a special display, you see a mannequin dressed as a hunter. It holds a bow and arrow—and not far from it you spot a huge trash container—with an arrow through its side. . . .

THE END

Taking a deep breath, you lunge forward, going down the steps in leaps and hoping you won't miss one. Just as the walls come almost together you reach the bottom and turn hard to the right. You find a large glass-windowed door with a huge handle. You grab the handle and try to shove it. But it won't give.

37

"It's got to!" you holler, and push with your shoulder. It remains tightly closed and you know the rear wall is going to crush you against the glass. Without hesitating, you jerk off a shoe and bang the glass. It shatters and cracks but does not give way.

"Break! *Please* break!"

Just as you begin to feel the pressure of the rear wall against you, the glass yields. You scrape both knees scampering through the opening.

You breathe a sigh of relief as you find a wide concrete floor, and you pause to catch your breath.

After a moment, you try to decide what to do. Ahead of you, well on the other side of the concrete floor, you spot a wall that appears to be lighted by a reflected glow. Off to your right is a narrow tunnel-like hall, totally dark except for a greenish light that appears to be leaking through cracks around a door. And barely to your left is a pitch-dark opening.

If you decide to go toward the reflected light, turn to page 88.

If you choose to go toward the green glow, turn to page 111.

If you think the totally dark opening is safest, turn to page 56.

38

You lurch forward, clutching the surface.

And just as you do, the belt begins to move, carrying you up. You don't know how it started—perhaps some workmen are on an upper floor and want to use it. But whatever the reason, you don't like being carried along this way.

Faster and faster the belt travels—with you hanging on desperately.

Then it stops with a squeal and you are thrown forward. Your head strikes a wooden wall and you are forced to turn around. This time, you fall on your stomach. But before you can move, a huge mechanical arm drops down and clawlike pincers grab you on both sides. You're lifted like a log and swished about in a half-circle.

The device suddenly stops, holds you poised for a moment, then drops you onto something thick and soft.

You lie perfectly still, hoping you have been placed on a pile of clothes or blankets.

Turn to page 17.

The mannequin moves again, stopping inches from your left side. As if on signal the mannequin dressed as a hunter moves also, stepping stiffly until it is directly to your left.

You swallow hard and want to back away or turn and run. But before you can move, the climber leaps at you, its left hand sweeping up and clutching you by the hair. The hard fingers scratch your skull, and you smell the distinct odor of damp plastic. The left arm rises and you feel yourself being lifted completely off the floor. It hurts and you scream loudly.

The mannequin begins to move with you toward the center of the floor, proceeding with wooden steps toward a huge support column. It halts within a foot of the structure and jiggles you for a moment. You glance down, and though it is almost totally dark, you can make out the thing's feet. The heavy boots have somehow sprouted one pointed spike at the toe of each—a spike at least two inches long. And you know they are sharp!

The climber kicks the support post with its right foot, raises the left and kicks once more. In quick jerks, the creature is climbing the column, easily carrying you along.

It proceeds to the top and you wonder about its balance. But it does not falter. It moves easily until it is within a foot of the ceiling. There it calmly takes

Turn to page 18.

40

Your body melts against the floor, you're so relieved. You hear the elevator banging about, then little pieces of wood and steel come tumbling down the shaft. When you can hear nothing more, not even the building settling, you creep to the opening and look up. All you can see is a dark sky, framed by the ragged edges of the roof. You breathe an exhausted sigh of relief and decide that for the next few minutes you'll just lie on the floor.

But before you have more than a moment to rest, you hear tiny scratching sounds. You whirl about and discover that you're in the toy department of the store. Wind coming down the elevator shaft has stirred one of the stuffed animals, making its little plastic claws scratch the surface of the shelf it sits on.

Turn to page 95.

You try to swallow, but the weight presses against your neck. Then you feel it once more; the springs begin to uncoil. The noise increases—and frighteningly you think you know why.

41

The coils are no longer springs. They're snakes and they are shaking their rattling tails. The springs sag in the middle, swell at both sides. And they are no longer in their original shape but are stretching, like snakes crawling and writhing. Wildly, you force a finger up, driving the nail into the surface of the mattress. Something gives! You jab harder!

Suddenly the fingernail forces its way through the covering. The water leaks briefly, then the sheer force of it tears the mattress apart.

You know you're going to be drowned. And if you're not drowned, the snakes beneath will bite through their covering and crawl all over the floor, all over you.

Turn to page 26.

42

But suddenly you open them wide. For a picture has appeared on the TV screen—a picture of *you* running through the store. As you stare, you see a huge man with a thick beard and great masses of black hair chasing you—and in his hand is a smoking pistol.

You sink lower in the chair, cringing as the picture moves. On the screen you duck behind a large pillar. The man fires at it and flakes of plaster fly off.

You scream—on the picture tube? Or where you're sitting?

The man gets much closer and you peek out from the hiding place. Once more he fires, this time knocking down a small picture hanging just above your head.

It's on the screen—but you feel it crash against your skull. Again he fires. This time the bullet strikes the ceiling and showers of plaster fall.

And still you feel it all about you—right there in the chair.

Continue.

On the screen you start to run. But you trip and fall on the floor. You cannot rise. The man laughs but it sounds like a raging howl. He cocks the gun. He aims. He shoots. Smoke comes from the end of the barrel.

And you slump against the back of the chair.

43

THE END

44

But now you hear more rattles, many more rattles, and you're certain that at least forty snakes are chasing you.

You find a decorator's pedestal that's round and much taller than you. It's about as big around as a small tree; frantically you grab it and you begin to climb. You reach the top and find a platform wide enough to crouch on. You balance yourself on it and peer through the fog, looking down.

Slowly, one by one, the snakes curl themselves around the pedestal and commence to climb after you, all now rattling their tails. You take off one shoe, bend as low as you can, and as they reach the platform you begin to beat their heads.

You beat and beat and beat. But one of them makes it to the platform behind you. You try, but you cannot turn around in time.

You lurch. The pedestal totters for a moment before falling down. And before you can do more than roll over, the snakes are all wrapped about your body. . . .

THE END

46

Again you listen. You continue hearing the sounds of things being moved about but you're sure they—whoever *they* are—didn't hear you. You wait a moment longer, but it dawns on you that the noise isn't coming from people moving things about. Huge motors that operate the escalators and elevators are simply cooling down after a day of running and heating up. Motors sometimes pop and crack and seem to scrape when they're getting cool.

Already exhausted from the tension, you decide you must rest awhile, and you have a sudden inspiration: Earlier, while you were wandering along one of the aisles, you overheard two clerks talking about the fashion show the store had had during the afternoon. You remember seeing a blue carpeted runway where the models had walked. At the farthest end, where they'd paused to turn around, there had been a white bear rug on the floor. Now *that* would be the best place to lie down.

Continue.

After several wrong turns, including one that put you right in the middle of a rack of silky dressing gowns, you find an open area. The runway. You drop down on your knees and begin crawling over the floor, feeling about. Your hand gropes in the darkness, and suddenly the smooth floor changes to something thick and furry. You bend close and peer hard. That's it. That's the bear rug, complete with declawed feet and a huge head with gleaming glass cycs and artificial tongue protruding from a gaping mouth.

47

Turn to page 104.

48

You roll over and over, hoping you won't drown. And as soon as you can jump to your feet, you run for the escalator steps. You scurry down them two and three at a time, and when you reach the next floor, you bound to the right—toward another wall. You work your way through a maze of counters and turn when you see a faint glow of reflected light.

Suddenly you find yourself in a row of look-alike dressing rooms. All the doors are open and you see nothing but a wall of tall mirrors. You pause at one and try to shake yourself dry. But all you do is fling a few drops of water on the mirrors.

Just a few drops—but that's enough.

You hear a sneeze and you stare. You don't believe it. But in all the mirrors, you see reflected ghostlike figures—men and women. At first, there seem to be only a few, but as you shake your head again, sprinkling more water onto the surfaces of the mirrors, more figures appear.

They are staring at the wall, at themselves, and at their reflections. Then they begin walking away.

It can't be. It simply can't be!

Turn to page 82.

49

You don't care what it does so long as it doesn't keep you bound. The moment you're free, you attempt to scamper away. But before you can get very far, you feel something cold digging into your back. Even without looking you know that Purgot has bent over and is gouging you with its long fingers. They are like the prongs of a large garden fork, except, unlike the garden tool, Purgot's fingers twist and turn.

They dig into your flesh, then probe from side to side. You feel them driving into your body, and you know Purgot is trying to get a firm and deadly grip on you.

Turn to page 51.

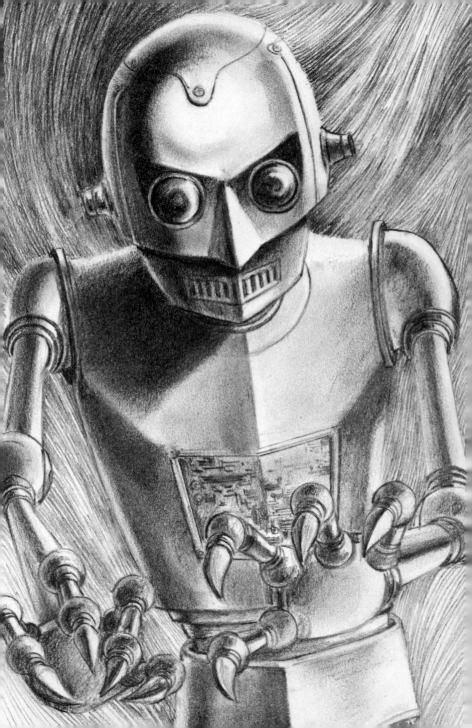

Despite all your efforts, the thing lifts you off the floor and holds you like a limp rag doll with one hand. With its other hand, it opens some kind of little door at the middle of its stomach and stuffs you inside.

You're wadded and squashed together like some kind of sponge.

Then you feel yourself being squeezed and you know what is taking place.

Purgot is shrinking back to its normal toylike size and you are being crushed within the metal box. . . .

THE END

52

You feel your way about and discover that you're standing next to a bed with no spread over it. You feel it. It's quite soft—much too soft for real comfort. But the very softness gives you an idea. You can raise the mattress and slip between it and the box spring. Even if the creature gets this far, it'll not be able to see you.

Turn to page 113.

The shape of a live bear!

You roll quickly off to one side as the huge head begins to wag. You cannot see too clearly but you know it's there—right beside you. And the breathing is now quite different. It's the low grunt of a real live bear.

53

You back away, trying to hide behind the first counter you can find. As you do, however, the bear's head turns. In your direction!

You'd better get away—fast. But if you run, you may catch the creature's attention, encouraging it to chase you. If you stay where you are, though, you'll be easy prey.

If you decide to run, turn to page 79.
If you decide to stay, hoping the bear won't bother you,
turn to page 68.

54

As the mattress swells, it begins to take the shape of a lopsided basketball. That gives you an idea. You doubt that the bed frame is put together permanently; more than likely, the foot is just barely supporting the box spring and mattress. If you can somehow extend your leg far enough, maybe you can get your big toe into the small framework and kick it loose. If you do, the water bed will roll off.

You struggle with all your might, and finally you're just able to touch something solid. You squirm against the weight that's pressing down and shove as hard as you can. At first nothing happens, but as the mattress continues swelling, the weight shifts. Your foot finds a corner of wood and you kick hard.

Good!

As you hoped, it gave way. The bottom of the bed drops and the huge water ball rolls off.

Have you escaped it? Turn to page 89.
If you flee, turn to page 103.

Reaching up without standing, you feel for the knob. When you find it, you hurriedly turn it and slip through the opening. The door slams shut.

55

You stand, gasping for breath—and discover that, instead of being outside as you'd hoped, you are in the beauty salon. The dim light shows the chairs, the sinks, the rows of shampoo on shelves, all sorts of curlers and blowers, and four huge chairs under dryers.

Well, if you can't get out, you can at least rest a moment.

You cross slowly to one of the chairs and let yourself down on the soft cushioned bottom. You lean back and sigh—

Then try to catch yourself as the chair suddenly tilts. You grab the arms, hoping to keep from sliding—but you slide, anyway, to a nearly prone position. A hose rises like a snake and squirts water all over your head. You shake it off and try to get up.

But before you can move away, a gigantic hood-dryer comes down over your head. And you are terrified as it begins to blow scorching hot air.

It dries your hair, your nose and mouth, your eyes, and your throat. You struggle to breathe—but the hot, stinging air has gotten into your lungs. And although you struggle, you go to sleep. A very long sleep . . .

THE END

56

Even though it is the darkest, you think perhaps the opening to your left may be the safest. Sometimes the most unexpected avenues turn out to be the very ones that offer help.

You hesitate only a moment before turning in that direction. You find a slight incline that seems to have small rollers across it; they remind you of some of the devices you've seen at stores where boxes are pushed along without being lifted.

Bending forward and putting your hand on it, you discover you are on a conveyor belt, and you attempt to climb it much as Hawaiians climb coconut trees. You move slowly, trying to keep your balance, and you think you're about halfway to somewhere, when you feel the belt suddenly jerk.

You grab for its edges.

It jerks again.

Turn to page 38.

Within minutes you hear noises outside. You can't be sure, but you think firemen are trying to knock down the door. As soon as you hear a good solid crash, you begin yelling. And you keep it up until you hear booted footsteps on the motionless escalator.

Three men in black waterproof suits come dashing across the floor, their brilliant flashlights illuminating the entire area. You holler for them and they spot you. One of them rushes to you and lifts you up. Without asking any questions, he hurries down the stairs and carries you outside.

The fire chief calls Uncle Jerry, who comes right over. "What happened?" he asks.

You know he won't believe you when you tell him about the alligator and the water bed. "I—I don't know," you mutter, "but I sure am glad to see you."

He puts you in the car and starts home. But you're so exhausted you fall asleep before you get there. . . .

THE END

58

You turn slowly, looking about, trying to discover just where you are—

Except that you cannot! There is no furniture, no clothing, no perfumes or housewares. You're in an empty room. And it has a frightening odor—like gas escaping from a broken pipe. The small safety lights are blinking on and off.

You've got to get out—but how?

You glance from one wall to the other—and are frightened by what you see. The very walls are shaking! Spinning around, you spot a heavy-looking green door. Hoping it's an exit, you run toward it. You grab the long barlike handle, and shove as hard as you can. It sticks—but only for a moment. And when it gives, you scurry through. The minute you release the door, however, it creaks and slowly closes itself—

Continue.

But you're outside! You can't believe it! On a wide sidewalk, near the parking lot. And there's a phone booth at the corner.

An hour later, you're at your uncle's house, fed, bathed, and in bed. The moment the lights are out, you fall asleep. Next morning when you wake up you just lie in bed for a while, recalling your experience in Wallenberg's. Absently you reach over and turn on the small bedside radio.

". . . And in the local news, workmen are already on the scene at Wallenberg's Department Store, surveying the damage caused when a wall collapsed during the night, destroying part of one floor. . . ."

THE END

60

Summoning all the courage you can muster, you decide to go downstairs.

You return to the escalator stairwell that you'd been on earlier, walk around it, and find the one that will take you to the basement floor. As you descend, you think you can see a little better because some light spills in through a display window in the sporting goods department.

You walk on tiptoe, however, because you don't want to be heard. If there's a burglar, you sure want to see him first.

You pass through the small cookware area and into the much larger hardware section. Even in the very dim light you see glints and reflections from shovels, small tools, and a row of large axes. You stop for a moment.

There—there's that noise again.

It seems to be coming from the toy department. You hesitate only a minute, then you sneak past the counters of nuts and screws, being very careful not to disturb anything that will give away your location. You move around a jutting panel that separates hardware from toys.

And once more you stop dead still.

You gaze about, hoping to find a swinging door or open window. The noise comes a third time. You instinctively turn toward it.

Continue.

No door. No window. Only the shelf of battery-operated toys. You squint your eyes, trying to locate the source of the sound. There at the end of the shelf you find it—a monster robot with a high forehead, arms that reach almost to its knees, a huge body, and short legs. Somebody left it turned on, and one of its dangling arms is striking an aluminum decoration as it moves back and forth.

You lift the robot from the shelf and place it on the floor to stop the noise. As your hand moves away, it becomes entangled in a string you didn't see. You attempt to jerk away, but the string knots about your finger. As you tug, a plastic two-foot-high human skeleton falls to the floor. You instinctively set it upright—and you notice its bones glow in the dark.

Oh, no . . .

The moment the two toys are on the floor, they begin to move. You understand about the robot—its battery still works. But you cannot see a switch on the skeleton.

They begin to move toward you.

Thoroughly frightened, you start to back away. They seem to get bigger and bigger.

Turn to Page 85.

62

Without standing, you reach up and grab the knob. You push hard—and find yourself in the wig department. But the minute you shut the door, you wonder if you'll be safe.

For no sooner has the latch clicked than you hear a scraping noise. You look up at the wigged heads on the shelves. Although their faces have no features, you *feel* they are all facing you. Again you hear the scraping sound, and this time you are sure it's coming from a small door at the opposite end.

You crouch, wondering what will happen next. The little door slowly opens and you see a shadowy figure emerge. You catch your breath, hoping it's not a burglar. The figure's arm extends to the left, as if reaching for something—a weapon—

And suddenly the room is brightly lighted. The figure becomes a man wearing a white jacket. He stares at you. *"What are you doing?"*

You tremble all over. "Mister—I went to sleep—all I want is to get out of this store!" Your lips have become dry and you lick them so they won't stick together. You explain about going to sleep, about not waking up until the store had closed.

Continue.

The man hesitates a moment, then slowly he smiles. He walks across the room and puts a gentle arm about your shoulder. "It's not the first time," he says. "Come along—we'll call you aunt and uncle." He opens a small sack and holds it toward you. "Meantime, how about a piece of candy?"

63

THE END

64

It will crash through the roof—you know it'll crash through the roof. And it will most certainly throw you out—it has no brake that you can find.

As it rises, you glance down at the bear's head once more—you don't know why.

And it's a good thing you do. Something seems to be—yes, something *is* crawling out of the open mouth and down the thick tongue. The something, you are horrified to see, is a huge round spider as big as a tennis ball. It gives off an amber glow like a bulb in Uncle Jerry's photographic darkroom. Its thin legs don't seem strong enough to support it, but as you stare you can see all of its insides.

Continue.

65

You watch as it begins to expand. It gets bigger than a volleyball, bigger than a basketball, and right there before your eyes it becomes the size of a massive beachball. Its glowing blood-red eyes roll right and left, sending out sharp little beams of light. For a moment the creature seems to be staring at the elevator floor. Then the gaze shifts up and up—until the pinpoints of light shine directly in your face.

You've never been stung or bitten by a spider, but you know some of them can kill. This one must have enough poison to kill ten people.

The elevator reaches the top and abruptly stops. Frantically you reach for the opening—but your hand strikes a blank wall. It's too high, way too high. But even while you're feeling your way, the elevator suddenly begins to drop. It plummets so fast that you're lifted off the floor.

If the spider starts to attack you, turn to page 99.
If you escape from the elevator, turn to page 105.

66

It slides along on the heavy base, scraping the tile floor as it moves. While you watch, frozen in your tracks, you feel heat rising from somewhere to your left. And you begin to hear more scraping sounds—

Four other dressmaker's forms are moving from the other side of the room. Three are armless but the fourth, like the first, has arms. The armed creatures move to either side of you before you can slip away. They grab you by the shoulders, lift you, and place you on the sewing machine. Two heavy sheets of cloth fall over you, and suddenly the machine begins to sew!

Before you can move, you're sewn inside a coarse sack. You struggle but cannot work yourself free. Then you're being lifted and moved—toward the source of heat.

You're placed on a flat surface that feels like an ironing board. You hear a heavy lever being pushed, a pedal being pressed down.

You scream—but the sound is muffled by the cloth. Then the steam presser comes down hard over your body, sizzling as it makes contact . . . .

THE END

As you squirm, one of the coils slips loose from the frame and jabs through the covering. It pricks your side and you try to yell. Try—but your voice is muffled.

67

Then a second breaks through, a third, a fourth, and a fifth. Another, another—and you lose count. One slips just beneath your ear and stabs the mattress.

But it is not water that comes out. As it trickles, then streams over your body, it feels like fiery acid, eating away at your flesh.

You scream but you make no sound.

The acid leaks into your nose, your mouth, your eyes and ears.

You scream again but you make no sound.

And as the burning acid eats through you, you frantically wish the alligator and Uncle Jerry would come find you. . . .

THE END

68

The heavy breathing turns into loud grunts, much louder than before, and the bear turns slowly. Even in the dark you are sure it spots you where you are cowering. It lets out a low rumbling roar, sways its massive head back and forth, licks its lips with the thick red tongue, and slowly rears up on its hind legs. When it stands all the way, you see that, even when you're standing on tiptoe, it's almost three times taller than you.

You swallow hard, shake all over, and gradually ease under the counter. The huge creature takes two steps toward where it last saw you, stands first on one rear foot, then on the other, almost doing a dance—death dance, you think—and roars a thunderous sound that fills the whole department store. With its left forepaw it swings mightily at the counter, and a loose box strikes a glass counter front ten feet away. The sound of broken glass angers the beast.

Once again it roars and thumps its chest, and you are convinced that its breath is like a tongue of fire. You drop to the floor, flat on your stomach, rolling to the left as you do so. But in the process your flailing right hand strikes the bear's foot. At once it moves back, bellows its anger, and crashes its forepaws on the countertop. The whole piece of furniture shatters like broken twigs and toothpicks, and there you are, exposed before him. You sit up, trying your best to

Turn to page 70.

70

slide backward while sitting down. You are able to move five, maybe six feet, then you can move no farther. Your back has come to rest against a rack of dresses stacked against the wall.

The bear, still moving on its hind legs, spies you and rumbles toward you, grunting all the way. It stops before you, pauses in its upright position, then bends forward, its forepaws outstretched, its claws extended. You've read about bears in the national forests and how they attack campers, tearing them to bits. You scream and scream and scream.

You wake yourself.

And you're still in the comfortable chair before the store's display of television sets. All the customers have left, the clerks are gone, and the only sounds you hear are vacuum cleaners being pushed along the aisles. Your scream, however, has attracted one of the cleaning people, a tall woman in a blue dress. She hurries over to where you are. "Lordy," she says, "what're you doin', still here?"

"I went to sleep, I guess," you say drowsily.

"Store's done closed. Want somebody to call your folks?"

Continue.

"Please," you answer.

And an hour later, apologizing to Uncle Jerry, you climb into the backseat for the short ride to their house. You hope, when you get to bed and go to sleep this time, you won't dream. . . .

THE END

72

More than anything else, you want to get outside, into the open air, and to a telephone where you can call Aunt Louise and Uncle Jerry—surely they're both home by now. Trouble is, you can't seem to find a way out.

And it's getting more and more frightening.

You try to think of some other possible way out and decide that, even though the escalators are behaving erratically, you must go downstairs. The building doesn't have windows; you noticed that when you first entered. But there are huge plate-glass displays at the storefront, and if window dressers can get to those to change the displays, so can you. You don't like the prospect of breaking such great panes of glass, but they appear to be your only avenue of escape.

Turn to page 23.

As well as you can remember, the rest rooms are against the far end wall, just past the alteration area. You wait until you are sure the alligator knows where you are, then you begin making your way through the racks of clothes toward the wall.

But the creature is smarter than you. As if sensing how you will proceed, it moves down an aisle and puts itself between you and the rest rooms. And it makes absolutely no sound.

Its silence frightens you. As long as you could hear those claw-feet padding over the carpet or scratching the tile, you knew where it was. But its soundlessness makes your spine tingle.

You stop dead still, hoping it will do something— even snort. But it's too smart for that. It suspects what you are doing and breathes very quietly.

On tiptoe you move past a table filled with pants on sale. You ease by a long counter which, you note, holds many different brands of shaving lotion—

Wait, now. There's an idea.

You feel along the glass top until your fingers touch a bottle of lotion. You don't care what it is, so long as it's strong. You gingerly open the top and sniff. Full.

Without hesitating, you throw it as hard as you can toward the ceiling. It breaks, shattering glass all over clothes and the floor. At once the air is filled with the aroma.

Turn to page 76.

74

Turning to your right, you spot a partition that separates furniture from a drapery section. You glance once toward the escalator landing, then spin and scurry past the partition. You move behind it and discover a wall of hanging drapes, curtains, and Venetian blinds.

A good place to hide!

You feel your way along until you touch what you believe is very heavy, very coarse material. It extends all the way from the high rods to the floor. Brushing back and forth, you find an opening and slip between two of the heaviest panels. There you lean back, thinking you'll discover a wall—

But it is not a solid wall.

Instead, it's composed of strong, wide slats, like a giant roll-up blind. And before you realize it, your foot becomes entangled in the draw cords. When you jerk about in order to free your heel, the catch slips loose—

Triggering the blind to rise.

Before you can even shout, it catches you, whips you about, and rolls upward like a gigantic shade, carrying you with it.

Continue.

And there you are—rolled up and bound, unable to move. And no matter how you struggle, you know you'll have to remain there until the store opens, until somebody comes to free you.

Still, you think to yourself, it's better than the jaws of the alligator. You can hear his claws scraping against the floor.

You smile.

THE END

76

The alligator snorts, then snorts again, and you know where it is. Right there at your feet!

You try to jump up, but your feet slip on a piece of glass and you fall not three feet from the 'gator. Its massive and treacherous head slowly turns toward you. Its glowing eyes fix on you. And this time, when it snorts, long tongues of fire erupt from its wide nostrils.

Not an alligator! A *dragon!*

You try to roll away but you bump into the legs of a table. You kick out but miss the beast's long snout.

The creature snorts again, and this time the flame scorches the soles of your shoes, burning through them and to the bare skin of your feet.

You scream at the pain but you kick again, anyway. The creature catches your foot and clamps down on it, its teeth sinking into your flesh. You fall back as the creature drags you toward the escalators and down and down, finally to the little fountain. It climbs in, dragging you with it, and takes you to the bottom of a deep, deep water pit . . . .

THE END

You dart to the left, heading—you hope—for the tools and workshop equipment. You are halfway there when you hear the whir once more. This time the arrow barely grazes your neck and crashes into the glass front of a wall display.

77

You make it to the aisles where the screwdrivers and pliers and hammers are. A third arrow barely misses your head, parting your hair as it zips past. Out of breath, you grab for the first small tool you can reach, spin about, and hurl it back at the hunter. You hear it hit something hard and bounce, but you know it didn't strike the mannequin.

Turn to page 35.

78

Perhaps you can puncture it and let the water out. You try a fingernail. It doesn't work. You force your fingers along the surface, feeling for a weak seam or maybe the filler tube. You find only a smooth surface.

The thing gets even bigger and you know you can't breathe much longer. Then suddenly something attracts your attention. The coils beneath you begin to move and change positions. And you hear a strange and frightening noise—it sounds like very small pellets shaking inside a little plastic box. The springs move more violently, as if they are alive.

If you think the springs will break through and puncture the mattress, turn to page 67.
If you believe the springs are "alive," turn to page 41.

It takes less than half a second for you to decide running away is the best solution. You whirl about, scrambling as you almost fall, and begin to run through the darkened mass of clothes racks and unexpected counters. Unable to see where you're going, you bang into a chair and fall on your face. You roll over—and there is the monstrous creature not three feet from you.

It has the advantage. It can see in the dark.

Vaguely, in the very dim light from the safety bulbs, you believe you see a large double-door exit. You can't tell what it leads to, but if it provides a way for you to leave this section and enter another, with a strong door you can close behind you, that's what you want.

You quietly run past a long rack of dresses, and just as it seems the beast will catch up with you, you reach the door.

You shove hard. It opens.

But instead of swinging the other way as you'd expected, it slides away to the left. No matter. You'll get away. You step past the door—only to discover too late that you've walked into the freight elevator!

And the bear can catch you now.

Frantically you slap at the walls beside the door— you are certain that somewhere along it there'll be a panel of buttons to make the elevator go up or down.

Turn to page 80.

80

Luckily you hit one, and even though it's dark, you can tell by the sudden and instant jerk that you have hit the DOWN button.

The elevator quickly begins to descend. But not before the bear leans toward you. You scream out, hoping with all your might that the creature doesn't step inside.

It doesn't!

Only its head comes within the elevator. The boxlike car drops rapidly. And as the top of it passes floor level, closing off the section you've been in, only the bear's head stays.

And it's severed at the neck!

The horrid thing falls to the floor and rolls into the far corner, rocks for a moment, then comes to rest facing you. The wide, glowing eyes are fixed on your body, and the thick tongue extends onto the floor.

You shake all over. But then you feel a sudden moment of wonderful relief. You don't like the terrible head, but you'd rather have it than the whole creature as a fellow passenger.

You think . . .

But just as you're beginning to relax, the elevator quickens its downward pace. You swing about, once more reaching for the control panel, hoping there's a STOP button you can push.

Continue.

You can't be sure what your finger hits, but abruptly the elevator stops, trembles, then just as abruptly begins to climb. You hit hard at all the control buttons but now none of them seems to work. And as the machine climbs, it seems to be going faster and faster.

Turn to page 64.

82

All the people who have used the dressing rooms have left their reflections. And the reflections are moving!

There is a difference, however. The heads on the reflected figures are weird, twisted, grotesque—long noses, eerie grins, eyes that are huge and frightening. Their mouths seem to be working although you hear no sounds. And when they move their lips back, their teeth are far, far too large!

The most horrid-looking one, a witch-faced woman with wrinkled cheeks, a bent nose, and protruding eyes, moves forward and points at you through the glass. Except that she seems much, much closer. She opens her mouth—

Continue.

And you hear her voice! "You have . . . disturbed . . . our disappearing . . . world. Now—you must join us!"

It doesn't make any kind of sense. You don't believe what you hear. But before you can move, the crone snaps her fingers. And hordes of others step from the mirrors. They surround you, their ghostlike arms lift you, and before you can do more than yell, "No, *no, NO!*" they carry you struggling through the glass. And you disappear into the mirrors . . .

THE END

84

You know you'd better run, so you reach behind, fumbling for the door handle. There is none—there is no way to open the door.

While you feverishly feel about for the space between the door and the wall, the witch breaks away from the angel and the rabbit, cackles a hair-raising laugh and skips toward you, stooping as she moves. "Got one, got one, got one!" her cracked voice seems to say. And before you can protect yourself, she grabs your arm, the bony fingers digging into your warm flesh.

You are dragged to the center of the ring and while the witch holds you in those bony claws, the angel and the rabbit viciously kick and scratch you.

"Death . . . death . . . death—death to Wallies, death to servers, death to buyers!"

You want to protest, you want to scream that you're lost, that you got locked inside the store and all you want is to leave. But your own shrill cry is lost in the din of their chant.

Turn to page 108.

The robot—its name, *Purgot,* is emblazoned in dark red across its forehead—turns right, turns left, fixes its attention on you, and commences to move forward, dragging its left leg as if somehow crippled. The skeleton also comes toward you, its bones rattling as it moves.

Within seconds *Purgot* is as tall as you are. Then it is taller than Uncle Jerry. And as it stalks you it sways from side to side, the huge form nodding, the protruding eyes staring down at the top of your head. Its arms are thick, its hands are huge, and its long fingers, you know, could wrap themselves about your throat with no effort.

The skeleton also grows, and though it has no eyes, the eye sockets appear to be turned on you. The joints and bones clack and grind, the fleshless feet clap the floor like well-timed rocks hitting a flat board.

"Stop!"

The sound of your voice echoes through the department store, but the things keep moving toward you. Terrified, you start to run.

If the skeleton catches you, turn to page 33.
If the robot is your antagonist, turn to page 102.

86

Without having a stick or rock or even a small chair handy to fight with, you begin rolling and rolling to the right because you remember seeing display tables in that area. You work your way beneath one, then another and another.

The alligator can see better in the dark than you can, however, and it begins to glide toward you. It moves quickly, its big head swinging from side to side and its tail slapping down displays one right after the other as it crosses the smooth tiled floor.

It's gaining on you.

Suddenly you spot the motionless escalator stairs. Forgetting that they might start up once more, you scramble to your feet and run as hard as you can toward them.

You hit them as fast as possible and begin climbing them two at a time. You are almost halfway up when you hear a *thump, thump, thump*.

Turn to page 6.

87

You struggle. The fingers dig even more fiercely into your flesh. You flail both arms, striking the fireplace, the edge of the mantel, the mannequin's hard shoulder.

The grip does not ease up.

Then, suddenly, as the figure leans closer to the flame to make certain the tip is held over the fire's hottest spot, you feel your feet touch a rise in the floor—the artificial fireplace's artificial hearth.

The creature seems not to notice.

And a frantic idea occurs to you. Why not shove the mannequin, spear and all, into the blaze?

If you decide to try and shove it into the blaze, turn to page 22.
If you choose another means of escape, turn to page 93.

88

The reflected light against the far wall seems to be the brightest, so you start toward it. You move cautiously at first, not trusting yourself. But when you feel the pavement is level, you hurry.

Moving ahead swiftly in the dark, you suddenly stumble down two steps that you had not noticed. You fall forward—and find yourself on very soft concrete, which feels as though it has just been poured.

Before you know it, your body is sinking into the wet concrete. You remember reading somewhere that the best thing to do if you fall into quicksand is to stretch out, covering a wide area, so that you don't sink as rapidly. But when you try this trick with the concrete it does not work. You feel yourself sinking deeper and deeper into the mirelike substance.

Holding your breath, you kick as hard as you can, flail your arms about, and roll first to one side, then to the other. And when you do, you find yourself sinking even faster.

You pass a small ledge and frantically reach for it, but your fingers slip off the edge.

Now you're going downhill. And ahead of you the light becomes brighter. Brighter—but suddenly warm.

You slide ten feet, twenty, thirty feet. And the farther you slide, the faster you go. Warm turns to hot. The glow does not come from lights—but from fire.

Turn to page 8.

But it doesn't simply come to rest. It wobbles crazily, as if controlled by a gigantic hand and is being pushed this way and that. Suddenly, before you've had time to do more than get to your feet, it begins to roll toward you. It's coming after you!

First it was the alligator. Now this thing. This *thing!*

You try to run, but you trip over another bed set. You slide off of it and stumble over a lamp cord you can't see. As you sprawl, the mattress rolls over your foot. You kick hard—

Then you can't jerk your foot away. Your whole shoe has somehow slipped through the small side handle used to lift the mattress. And as the ball rolls, it lifts you and begins to throw you helter-skelter.

Turn to page 91.

90

One of the transistors, longer than the others, moves from right to left, pauses, then settles in the center of the screen. Its glow changes from blue to green, from green to orange, then it begins to wriggle as if alive.

The screams intensify, reaching such a peak that the noise fills the whole of the fourth floor. Something is about to burst—you know it.

Suddenly the sound dies away. The wriggling light changes shape, curls and coils and knots itself. And you recognize what it is—you've seen things like it on television many times: it is a hangman's glowing noose.

You swallow hard and instinctively put your hand to your throat.

But you're too late.

The picture tube cracks, showering the floor with glass fragments. And before you can rise, the noose comes hurling at you. It circles your head, drops down and around your neck, and in an instant you are jerked screaming into the television set. . . .

THE END

You scream and reach for the handle. But before you can grasp it, the thing has rolled you under itself and continued on toward the opposite end of the department. Lamps and small tables, chairs and bookcases are knocked aside and shattered.

You scream, although you're sure by now nobody else is in the store. Your ankle is beginning to hurt, your stomach has been mashed so hard you think it won't ever be right again, and you are afraid that if the thing keeps throwing you about it will bash your head against something hard and deadly.

It pauses once, teetering first one way, then another, and in that instant your flailing hands catch something on the floor. You can't be certain, but you think it is one of those long-handled outdoor forks, the kind people use when they're barbecuing steaks in the backyard. You twist about, hoping it is a fork, and jab the side of the ball.

Instantly it explodes, showering you and the furniture with gallons and gallons of water.

Are you about to get away? Turn to page 32.
If you think about running, turn to page 48.

92

Hesitating only a second, you slip off a shoe and hold it out toward the huge creature. It pauses a moment before moving closer. You jiggle the shoe. It eyes your hand, its vicious jaws working up and down. You stretch as far as you can, trying to keep yourself at more than arm's reach.

Suddenly it lunges. The shoe falls onto the floor with a soft thump. The alligator grabs you by the arm. You yell and spin about and kick it as hard as you can, right under the lower jaw—in the throat, you hope. It releases you, wags its mighty head back and forth, then abruptly lowers itself to the floor.

And while you watch, it begins to shrink! It keeps getting smaller and smaller until it's no larger than the iguana you saw much earlier in the evening. You watch as it very slowly turns around, inches its way back to the fountain, and returns to its rock.

Turn to page 107.

The idea may be intriguing, but right now all you're interested in is getting away. You remain still, waiting until the creature is totally concentrating on heating the spear tip, then you lunge as hard as you can. You are lucky—you break from its grasp. And once your feet hit the floor, you don't stop running until you're on the far side of the department.

You duck around a tall partition—and find yourself in the luggage department. You work your way past rows of suitcases and overnight bags, not stopping until you are safely hidden behind a huge black trunk. You relax a moment and lean against it—

And it moves!

It moves, and you hear a thumping sound coming from inside. Can't be! Can't be anything in there.

The thump comes again. And you think it's some kind of code—as if somebody—or something—might be tapping out a signal.

The idea frightens you, but if somebody else is trapped in the store besides you, a companion would be nice. Cautiously you tap the surface. At once the inside tapping becomes louder, harder, and faster. Like dot-dash-dash-dot—

Someone is there!

You fumble with the clasp, click its fastener, and slowly lift the lid—

93

Turn to page 94.

94

But before you can make another move, a huge hairy arm reaches out, grabs your wrist, and jerks you inside. The lid closes. You scream—but a shaggy creature wraps its mighty arms about you . . .

THE END

Being in the toy department reminds you that you're not too far from the sporting goods. You think hard and vaguely remember seeing a large display window that looks out on the lower-level parking area.

And if it looks out in that direction, there must be a way to break through and escape this weird building.

Feeling your way, you bump and stumble to where you remember seeing the window. At first you bang into a wall, then into a row of shelves filled with fishing tackle. But once you step around it, you can move directly to the window. It's just as you re-called—a large window with three dressed manne-quins. One of the males is wearing camouflaged hunting gear, and in his hand is a large bow. The second male is wearing mountain-climbing gear, complete with knife and long rope. The female is dressed in a scuba outfit, with back tank, and under-water fishing spear.

You move closer and are almost there when you are startled by a rustling sound. You strain hard and look at the area where the mannequins are posed. First, the hunter slowly pivots, then the diver, and finally the climber. And as you stare, almost petrified by what you see, they aim their weapons at you—the bow and arrow, the long knife, and the fishing spear!

If you're too terrified to move, turn to page 16.
If you elect to spin about and run, turn to page 9.

96

The female mannequin stops inches from your left side. As if on signal, the mannequin dressed as a mountain climber moves also, stepping stiffly until it has positioned itself at your right.

You swallow hard and want to back away, to turn around and scramble somewhere else. The hunter does not move. You set yourself, tense your muscles, and suddenly spin on your left heel. The mannequins do not move from their fixed positions. You let out a yell and run as hard as you can.

You are almost at the toy department when you hear a sharp, low, whistling sound and feel something brush past your shoulder. You stop abruptly, realizing the hunter mannequin has shot an arrow at you. It buries itself in a huge stuffed lion.

Now you understand! The mannequin is hunting his prey . . . and it's you. Most hunters like the thrill of the chase, and he was simply waiting to pursue you.

Do you keep running? Turn to page 77.
Or should you hide? Turn to page 106.

You scream at it to go away but it continues to pursue you. You crawl from the support pillar toward where you remember the staircase is—the useless escalator. But by now you're almost exhausted. You think you can go no farther, that if you try to move another foot you'll simply collapse.

Hey, that's an idea!

Collapse. Lie flat on your back. Pretend you are asleep. Or dead.

You ease yourself down onto the floor and stretch out full length. You roll over on your back, fix your stare straight up at the ceiling, and do not move.

But out of the corner of your eye you see that the skeleton is not to be so easily deterred. It towers above you for a moment, then slowly crumples to the floor. Strangely, it lies down beside you, stretching flat on the floor just as you have done. And something else—

It shrinks.

It shrinks until it is exactly your height.

And then you feel yourself become lighter and lighter. Parts of you begin to move away, to disappear. And very gradually, while you can do nothing to stop it, most of your body transfers from your skeleton to the plastic one.

Turn to page 98.

98

Within minutes, *you're* a skeleton. Only your brain is left. The rest of you has turned the plastic thing into a fully developed body. . . .

THE END

Both you and the spider are for the moment suspended within the falling elevator. You claw at the air, desperately trying to find the wide handrail or the control panel or anything else that will allow you to get away.

You touch nothing.

And when you do fall to the floor once more, the eye-lights are focused on your neck. You can barely make out the spider's menacing form, but you can tell by the glow that it is moving nearer. You slap at

Turn to page 101.

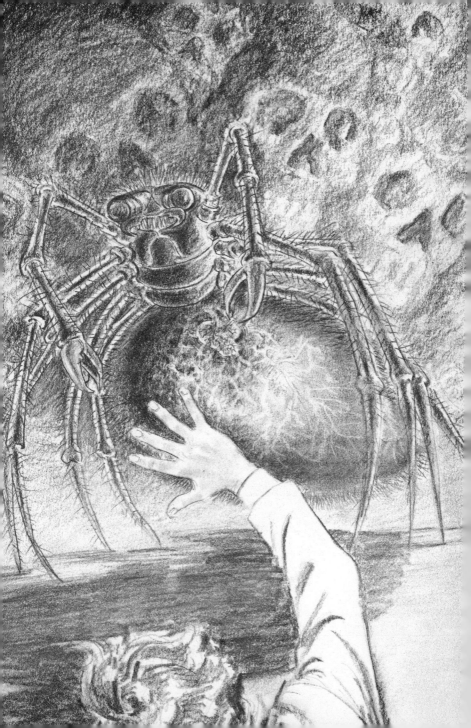

it. You grab for the elevator walls. You kick out, doing your best to scoot along the unsteady floor. But whatever you do, whichever way you attempt to move, the glowing eyes stay fixed.

And the creature moves on its spindly legs. The massive form is too close, and as you stare at it you think you can see through the translucent body—you find yourself gazing almost hypnotized at the rapidly beating heart.

You stare because you cannot help it.

And you are still staring when the monstrous spider bites you on the side of the neck.

Suddenly you cannot move. You are totally paralyzed, but your eyes can see. . . .

THE END

102

You make your way around the end of a display table, reaching out and hoping to find some kind of tool—you think you've retreated into the store's hardware department. However, your fingers rub uselessly over a cardboard box and you know that it offers no help. You stumble. Your foot catches on the leg of a workbench and you trip and fall onto the floor.

Purgot pauses long enough to nudge you in the side with its hard metal toe. You scramble to your knees and try to crawl backward.

Desperately you yell, "Stop!"

Somehow the sound of your voice triggers a mechanism within Purgot that you had not expected. It, too, has a voice. It throws back its head and roars a mighty roar, setting the whole floor vibrating.

You attempt to spin about and move forward; anybody can crawl faster forward than backward. But your feet become entangled in some electrical cord and you have the sinking feeling that you can't jerk free. Finally you tug with all your might. The cord is pulled from its socket and flies about like a water hose that has just been turned on.

Turn to page 49.

Without waiting to see what happens to the thing, you scamper off the springs and run headlong through the semidarkness. You bump into a lamp, then you trip over a small ottoman. You scramble to your feet and keep running.

You reach a small door and without waiting to see where you may be, you dash through it and slam it behind you. For a moment you pause and lean against it, catching your breath. And while you do, you look around. There is virtually no light in this room, but you can tell by the forms before you that you've somehow gotten into the alterations room. You see what you believe is an ironing board, three large sewing machines, and a form—

You stare at the form. It's shaped like a body, set on a long pipe, with no legs, no head. It's one of those models dressmakers fit pieces of cloth on when they're making a dress or suit—

Hey!

It has arms. Things like that don't have arms!

But it does.

And before you can take another deep breath, the arms suddenly reach out. One of them flips a switch and you hear a motor come to life. One of the sewing machines has been turned on.

Before you can do more than glance at it, the crazy form moves toward you.

Turn to page 66.

104

You ease over onto it, trying to make certain that you're right in the center of it. You test the fur, find that you've gotten to the most comfortable area, and let yourself down. At first you lie on your stomach, but the fur tickles your face and you turn over. Once on your back, you relax and close your eyes. Uncle Jerry or Aunt Louise will call the store manager or the police or somebody and they'll come looking for you. But you're too tired to think about that—

Hey!

That sounds like somebody breathing.

You hold still, not daring to move a muscle.

There it is again. Some*thing* or some*body* breathing. And not far from where you are.

And something else. You know the bear rug is on the floor and the floor is flat as can be, but you begin to feel a lump. Then, not just a lump but a long pole, except that it's not straight and not even a pole— more like a crooked limb from a tree. And it's right beneath your back.

And it's slowly beginning to move.

You try to turn over quickly but you're so frightened you cannot make your muscles move.

Turn to page 27.

Both you and the spider bounce up and down for a moment, then it begins to move slowly toward you, its eye-lights fixed on your legs. The elevator continues plummeting and you are sure that it will crash this time. You think it might be better for this to happen than for the spider to bite you.

Just as the elevator reaches what you believe to be the bottom, it suddenly slows down, then comes to a quick stop.

The basement floor!

Without waiting, you spin toward the hoped-for opening and dive through. And just in time, for no sooner have you gotten through and onto the tiled floor than the elevator begins to rise once more. You can tell by the sounds that it is moving faster and faster—you hear the motors whine and the cables pop. And this time it does not stop. With an ear-splitting crash it bangs through the building's roof, carrying the gigantic spider with it.

If you think you're safe now, turn to page 40.
If you expect another trap, turn to page 118.

106

You believe your only chance is to drop to the floor and crawl away, using counters to shield you. Without hesitating, you fall to your knees and head away from the mannequin. And it seems that you've crawled half a block when you crash into a door.

A door! A way to escape!

If you think the door leads outdoors, turn to page 55.
Or does it take you elsewhere? Turn to page 62.

You breathe a sigh of relief. For a moment you were sure you were going to be bitten into pieces, probably eaten. You touch your arm where the terrible teeth grabbed you. There are small scratches and little indentations where the sharp teeth points dug in, but you're not bleeding.

You are still thinking how close you came to being a meal for the alligator when you hear the strangest kind of noise coming from somewhere below you. You catch your breath, straining to hear it better.

There it goes again.

This time you think you recognize the sound. A big door is being opened and its hinges are making a most unusual squeak.

A door opening?

Somebody down there?

If somebody is downstairs, maybe he or she can tell you how to get out of the building. On the other hand, maybe it's a burglar — people often break into big stores at night, even stores that have excellent burglar alarms.

You want to go down there, hoping it's somebody who can let you out. But you hesitate because it could be a burglar.

If you decide to go downstairs, turn to page 60.
If you think it best to go elsewhere, turn to page 7.

108

Then, above the noise of the shattered creatures, comes a roar from the distant, darkened corner. The sound sends cold chills up and down your spine. The creatures turn.

From the darkness emerges the hugest, ugliest ogre in the world—its skin is like old wrinkled leather, its neck stretches up and down as it moves, its apelike nostrils flare, and its orange eyes shower sparks as it clumps toward you.

"One of them, one—one!" the creatures voice in hoarse unison. "Of the Wallies!"

Turn to page 110.

110

You protest. You scream. You try to jerk free. But before you can move, the angel rushes to the rubbish pile and fetches a frayed electrical cord. Hastily the creatures bind you, tying your legs together, your hands behind your back. You attempt to protest again but the witch rams a sodden cotton ball in your mouth.

"Death, death, death!"

The ogre lets out a roar that clearly tells you this is their executioner. And it moves your way. The rabbit, the angel, and the witch fall back. The ogre towers above you and bends its monstrous head, its eyes trained on your stomach. The ogre's mouth opens wide, exposing double rows of inch-long saber teeth. And you almost begin to scream . . . except you're silenced too quickly.

THE END

Even though the hallway to the right is quite narrow, you select it because the greenish light that leaks from the door makes you think people are there—somebody who can help you get out of the building.

And when you are close to the door, you do begin to hear peculiar noises. They sound like voices . . . but not quite.

You touch the door and it swings easily inward. You enter and at once the door slams shut. A distinct click tells you it has latched itself.

You move forward only a couple of steps. And abruptly stop. Before you, spread in a circular disarray, are more holiday decorations than you have ever seen—all broken. A fractured plastic turkey without its head, limbs of artificial Christmas trees, shattered red valentines, yellowing Easter lilies strewn about the floor, strings of tree ornaments piled in a tangled mass, twisted and disfigured horns of plenty, and countless dismembered Santas.

In the center of the circle of once-festive litter are a furless rabbit, a wingless angel, and a hatless witch. They are holding hands (or paws), hopping about in a circle. And though the sounds are very indistinct, you make out words. "Death, death, death—"

Turn to page 28.

112

But suddenly you open them wide. For there on the TV screen, moving as if alive, are all the electrical parts of the set. Tubes, wires, connectors, and transistors are swirling about in a gray background, lighted by a leftover glow from the earlier electricity.

As you stare, they begin to explode into huge balls of blood-red fire. And each time one bursts, you hear a faint scream, as if someone behind the set is being hurt.

You sit forward, muscles tense and arms shaking.

A flame ball bounces around within the picture tube, clacking as it strikes the glass. Each time it strikes, the mysterious scream becomes louder. You slip forward to the edge of the chair, looking right and left, wondering if the whole thing will blow up.

Turn to page 90.

As you lift the mattress's corner you hear the distinct *thump, thump, thump* of the 'gator's claws. It has climbed all the way to the fourth floor, too, and is stalking you!

Hastily, you lift the mattress and work yourself onto the spring, taking every precaution not to make it squeak. You shuffle yourself beneath the mattress, cautiously pulling in both feet so you're totally covered, then you turn your head to the side, just enough to breathe through the tiny crack between the two pieces of bedding.

But you can still hear the alligator.

It's somehow trailing you and you wonder if it is able to smell people the way bloodhounds can.

Then it seems to stop and all you can hear is the swish-scraping noise of the huge tail moving back and forth. Suddenly that stops for barely an instant.

Then *crash!*

The mannequin.

The creature has slapped at the male mannequin with its powerful tail, breaking the thing apart and sending it crashing across the floor.

Then you hear the little claw-feet moving once more. They get louder and louder and you're sure it has tracked you to the very place you decided was safe.

Turn to page 114.

114

But just as you're about to slip out the other side and try to run, the sounds pause. The tail stops swishing. The frightening jaws cease clacking. There's an eerie snort, then another, and a third.

And while you're still trying to make up your mind about running once more, you hear the claws scraping across the floor. You hold your breath and listen. It's turning around. The alligator is turning around as if it has given up the chase!

You stay as still as you can, hardly breathing, daring not to make any move that would cause the mattress to shift or the springs to squeak.

The claw-steps move away and—lucky, lucky you—they seem to be retreating toward the escalator stairs once more.

You do not move until the sounds have completely stopped, when you're certain that the creature has descended at least to the third floor and, you hope, all the way to the first.

You decide to ease out from under the protective cover of the mattress.

Except when you try to move, you discover that it's not so easy. For a reason you cannot understand, the mattress is much heavier than it was at first.

You push it with your open palm.

Continue.

And that's when you realize why it was so soft. It's not a regular matress, as you had first thought, but one of those water beds. And it's much tighter on the surface than it was earlier. Tighter and very much heavier.

Its weight begins to press down on you and you *know* it was not like that when you first slipped beneath it.

It's swelling. That's what it's doing—it's swelling.

It seems to get heavier and heavier and the covering becomes so tight that you can hardly make a depression in it—not even with your fist.

Turn to page 31.

116

You take a step back, then another and another. You pause just a moment before spinning on your heel—whatever these creatures mean to do, you want no part of it. You intend to run.

Before you can make a start, however, one of the diver-mannequin's plastic arms reaches out and grabs you about the back of the neck. The icy grip of those fingers sends a chill down your back and the hard tips dig into your flesh. You cannot believe it. The mannequin almost lifts you off the floor and carries you without effort past all the sporting equipment and through the hardware section to the area set apart for all kinds of heaters.

She leads you past a camp stove, a large wood burner, and a row of electrical units, not halting until she reaches an artificial fireplace with a long gas log set inside.

Still holding on to your neck, she bends over and touches a small button. Instantly flames leap up about the log—blue-white gas jet flames that grow and grow until they blend into an orange loglike fire. The heat is immediately fierce, and you wonder if the fire will set the store burning.

Or you. . .

The mannequin bends forward slightly, extending the underwater fishing spear toward the blaze.

Continue.

And suddenly you understand. She means to heat the tip to a flesh-burning glow. And then she intends to shoot you with it.

Turn to page 87.

118

As soon as you catch your breath, you get off the floor and work your way through the toy department, looking once more for a door that may let you out. You pass through the hardware displays, still barely able to see, and turn down a short aisle. You come to a low, batwing door and ease through it.

You're in the store's small cafeteria. You smell food, and that reminds you that you haven't eaten for quite a while.

You step behind the long serving counter and feel your way toward the kitchen. At the counter's end you come to a heavy service door that seems to be stuck. Pushing hard, you go through the opening— and the door closes with a hard scratch. Never mind—the refrigerator has to be nearby. You feel along the wall, touching cabinet doors and the edge of the sink. And just when you believe you've found what you're looking for, you hear a sudden hissing noise.

You stop, holding your breath.

There it is again. And when you turn toward it, you see a green glow. The giant coffeepot. It should have been turned off, but apparently somebody forgot. Inside the huge tank the water is gurgling.

Turn to page 29.

You yell and scream, kick and push. Nothing helps. The machine completely wraps you in the thick, quilted fabric, slows down, then stops altogether. Once more you're moved—down. And you feel yourself being slipped into a container.

You're being stuffed inside a box!

Another machine pushes you tightly into the container. Then you hear hammers driving nails.

Then nothing.

And you know you're wrapped up, nailed inside a wooden box, standing head down. Ready to go . . .

THE END

120

You land in a row of thick, untrimmed hedges that surround the building.

You're dazed. You're scratched all over. You think perhaps you are bleeding but you don't care—you're out. You're out!

Trembling all over, you scramble to your feet and cross the parking lot, past the dimly lighted little turnaround areas, past the restraining curbs, past a row of neat trees that appear to surround the entire area. And you do not stop until you reach a wide, grassy stretch of ground separating the huge Wallenberg's site from the nearby avenue.

The grass is tall and you fall in it. You lie there gasping for air. Your head spins, your stomach churns, and when you turn your head your throat burns.

You decide to lie in the grass for a while. It's safe. Nothing more will come after you. And even if it does, you're in the dark. You can easily hide.

But you're so tired you don't want to move. You're so sore you don't want to feel anything, do anything.

You remain on the cool, damp grass longer than you think. Finally you rouse yourself and turn around to look at the building.

Except you discover, when you glance about, that there is no parking lot, there is no fire, there is no building. Nothing at all. You are standing in a vast

Continue.

field of tall, thick grass. You see no lights, hear no automobiles, feel no breeze at all.

With trembling fingers you put your hand to your face. There is no blood, only dew from the grass.

You move your feet slowly, hoping that you are still able to walk. They stumble over the ground, but they move at your command.

As you stand there wondering which direction to turn, wishing you could see a light, names pass through your mind. But all are quite vague—except two.

The names Uncle Jerry and Aunt Louise keep slipping in and out of your consciousness, and you wonder why. . . .

THE END

Books in our

PLOT-YOUR-OWN HORROR STORIES™

Series!

CRAVEN HOUSE HORRORS #1
by Hilary Milton

NIGHTMARE STORE #2
by Hilary Milton